Postman Pat

and the Toy Soldiers

Story by John Cunliffe

Pictures by Ray Mutimer

From the original Television designs by Ivor Wood

Hippo Books
Scholastic Children's Books
London

Scholastic Children's Books,
Scholastic Publications Ltd,
7-9 Pratt Street, London NW1 0AE, UK

Scholastic Inc.,
730 Broadway, New York, NY 10003, USA

Scholastic Canada Ltd,
123 Newkirk Road, Richmond Hill,
Ontario, Canada L4C 3G5

Ashton Scholastic Pty Ltd,
PO Box 579, Gosford, New South Wales,
Australia

Ashton Scholastic Ltd,
Private Bag 1, Penrose, Auckland,
New Zealand

First published by André Deutsch Children's Books 1991
An imprint of Scholastic Publications Ltd.

This edition published by Scholastic Publications Ltd. 1993

Text copyright © 1991 by John Cunliffe
Illustrations copyright © 1991 by Scholastic Publications Ltd.
and Woodland Animations Ltd.

ISBN 0 590 55170 1

Printed by Proost International Book production

They were having a busy summer in Greendale.

Alf was getting the hay in.

There was something of a traffic jam in the middle of the village. Pat had left his van outside the post-office. And *someone* had left a lorry on the other side of the road. It was a tight squeeze. Alf got stuck trying to squeeze through with his tractor. And then Miss Hubbard came along, and called out, "What's all this, Alf? Mustn't block the road, you know!"

3

Then out came Mrs. Goggins from the post-office.

"What's to do?" she said. "Don't take on now. Pat'll be back in a minute to move his van, when he's done the village letters."

"It's this lorry!" said Miss Hubbard. "Who's left it here? There's no sign of a driver!"

Peter Fogg came along on his motorbike.

"What's going on?" he said. "Has there been a crash?"

"There will be if this lorry isn't moved," said Miss Hubbard.

"It looks like a builder's lorry," said Peter.

No one saw P.C. Selby, behind the load of hay.
"Now then, now then, what's going on?"
Oh dear . . . P.C. Selby *was* looking cross.
"You can't block the road like this, you know."
They all talked at once . . . what a mix-up!
"Now then, let's get things sorted out," said P.C. Selby.

5

All this time Pat was hurrying round with the letters for the village.

"Pat!"

It was Sara, calling and hurrying after Pat, with a parcel in her hands.

"It must be your forgetting-day, Pat," said Sara. "You went off without your sandwiches. Here we are. Special delivery!"

"Just like a parcel!" said Pat. "I'd better not pop them in somebody's letter-box by mistake!"

"You'll be hungry, if you do," said Sara. "Bye!"

They still hadn't sorted out the traffic-jam outside the post-office. P.C. Selby was waving his hands about, and shouting to Alf, "Left a bit . . . right . . . RIGHT . . . NO . . . RIGHT!"

Alf was going to and fro with his tractor, but he seemed more stuck than ever. Everyone else tried to help, but they only made it worse.

"You've got me all of a smuzzle!" said Alf. "I'm staying put till somebody moves that lorry!"

Then Ted Glen and Major Forbes arrived.

"Hang on," said Ted. "I'll just move the lorry."

So *that's* who caused the traffic jam! Ted Glen! Now Major Forbes waved his arms about, and tried to explain to everyone.

"So sorry, everybody," said the Major. "Ted's just giving me a hand at the Hall. Borrowed the lorry . . . first traffic-jam in Greendale, *what*! Soon be off . . ."

And now here comes Pat.

"Morning everybody!"

"Just a word, Pat," said the Major. "Urgent parcel . . . coming from London . . . bought these tin soldiers for my collection . . . now take good care of it, there's a good chap, *what*!"

"Don't you worry, Major," said Pat. "I'll see you get it, safe and sound, the way you always do."

"Good man . . . Bye for now!"

And Major Forbes was off with Ted in the lorry. At last, Alf could get on his way. And Miss Hubbard . . . and Peter . . . and everyone else.

Mrs. Goggins still had the country parcels and letters to sort, and Pat went to help. But, oh dear, there were two parcels with no address. Mrs. Goggins found a label that had come unstuck.

"It's this modern glue," said Mrs. Goggins. "They're for ever dropping off. Now which one shall I put it on?"

"I think it belongs to that one," said Pat.

"But that leaves one without an address," said Mrs. Goggins.

"Don't worry," said Pat. "As soon as somebody says – 'Where's my parcel?' – I'll know it must be theirs. Simple!"

"I'd never have thought of that. Goodbye, Pat. Mind how you go!"

"Bye!"

"Now then, Jess," said Pat. "We'd better take the Major's parcel first. It's something special. Toy soldiers."

Pat was on his way.

When Pat arrived at Garner Hall, there were builders' things everywhere, and the sound of hammering, but no sign of Major Forbes.

"Looks as though the Major's busy," said Pat. "Anybody at home?"

The hammering went on, but no one answered.

"Hello . . . Major? It sounds as if he's putting on a new roof . . ." said Pat to Jess.

He rang the bell. No answer.

He knocked. No answer.

He opened the door. No one about.

He called again.

"Hello-o . . . hello, Major! Ted!"

Still there was no answer.

11

What could Pat do?

"I know," said Pat, "I'll just leave his parcel on this table. It'll be quite safe here. Where is everybody? They must be having a tea-break."

Pat closed the door carefully and went on his way.

There were some letters for Dr. Gilbertson.

"It's a good thing you called, Pat," said the Doctor. "Granny Dryden needs some more ointment for her rheumatics. Now if you could just call by . . ."

"It'll be a pleasure," said Pat. "I'll be passing the door."

Jess hoped it was something good to eat.

"No, it's not for you, Jess," said Pat. "Cats don't get rheumatics, do they?"

Pat was on his way.

Granny Dryden was delighted to see Pat.
"Just what I need for my poor old bones,"
she said. "Are you any good at mending
blocked sinks, Pat?"

"Well, I'll have a look and see what I can
do . . ." said Pat. "I'll see if I have a spanner
in the van."

When Ted tried to get his lorry past Pat's van there was another
traffic-jam. So Ted came looking for Pat in Granny Dryden's
kitchen. Oh, dear, what was Pat up to? He was on his knees, in a pool
of water, with water dripping and splashing and spurting all over the
place.

"What are you doing, Pat?" said Ted. "Are you making a
swimming-pool for Granny Dryden?"

"It's just a blocked sink . . ." said Pat.

"It looks like a blocked waterfall to me," said Ted. "I'll tell you what, Pat. You get your van out of the way, and *I'll* see to this sink."

Pat was glad to leave Ted to mend the sink. He was good at that kind of job.

Pat was on his way.

When lunch-time came, Pat said,
"Let's have a picnic, Jess."
   They found a cool place to sit,
under a tree, and Pat opened
his parcel of sandwiches.
Well . . . he *thought* it was his parcel of sandwiches . . . but the
sandwiches felt very hard and heavy and knobbly. When he
unwrapped the paper, what a shock he had!
   "Oh, no! *These* aren't my sandwiches!" wailed Pat. "They're the
Major's toy soldiers! How did they get into my lunch? Oh, what a
noodle I am! I've got the wrong parcel! I must have left my
sandwiches on the hall table in the Major's house. It must have been
this parcel that the address fell off! Come on, Jess. Back to the
Major's! He'll be thinking his soldiers have run away!"

When Pat arrived back at Garner Hall, there was the Reverend Timms trying to cheer the Major up, and P.C. Selby was looking for footprints.

"What's going on?" said Pat.

"Robbery," said the Major. "That's what's going on, Pat. All the rest of my collection of soldiers . . . gone . . . all gone, *what*! Marched off without a sound. But there's a funny thing. The robbers left their sandwiches behind!"

"Oh, no . . ." said Pat, "they were *my* sandwiches . . . You see, I muddled the parcels up – my sandwiches and your soldiers – I left my sandwiches on your hall table, and your parcel of soldiers was still in my bag. And here it is!"

"You're a genius, Pat!" said the Major. "You've saved my new soldiers from the robbers, *what*! The best of the bunch, too! Good man."

"But I'm still hungry," said Pat.

"The Lord will provide," said the Reverend Timms.

"I'll just pop in for my sandwiches," said Pat.

"Now then, Pat," said P.C. Selby, "I'll have to ask you for a Statement. And you can't go in there, Pat . . . not till we've looked for finger-prints."

"But I want my sandwiches," said Pat.

"Those sandwiches are Evidence," said P.C. Selby. "Evidence, Pat, that's what they are. We can't have you eating the Evidence, now can we? There might be finger-prints on them, you know. Nobody's allowed to touch them. Not till the CID get here from Pencaster, and goodness knows when that'll be."

"I wonder if Sara's got something nice for lunch," said Pat. "I'm *so* hungry. I think we'll have to pop home and see, Jess."

So Pat went home for his lunch. When Sara saw him coming through the door, she said, "You've never lost your sandwiches, after all, have you?"

"Not *lost*," said Pat, "but they're Evidence, now."

"Well, I never . . ." said Sara. And Pat had to tell her the whole story of the robbery at Garner Hall and the mixed-up parcels.

Sara found a nice slice of pizza for Pat's lunch. When he had finished, he said, "I'll have to be on my way. There are still lots of letters to be delivered, robbery or no robbery."

"Now you'll be passing the school just about the right time to pick young Julian up," said Sara. "Save me a trip."

"All right! I'll not forget!" said Pat. "Bye for now!"

Pat was on his way.

He had a magazine for Miss Hubbard, and stopped to tell her all about the robbery.

"What a day you must have had," said Miss Hubbard. "What you need is a drop of my best elderberry cordial. Come along, Pat, and tell me all about it."

It was a lovely glass of cordial.

"That was nice," said Pat.

Pat was on his way.

He met Peter Fogg at the side of the road, trying to mend his motorbike.

"Having trouble, Peter?" said Pat.

"I certainly am," said Peter. "My chain's come off . . ."

"I'll ask Ted to pop along with his tool-kit," said Pat. "Here's something to read while you're waiting."

"Ooh, good, it's my motorbike magazine," said Peter. "Great! Bye, Pat! And thanks!"

Pat was on his way.

He called at Thompson Ground.

Alf was helping Ted to load some wood on to the lorry. They stopped to see what Pat had brought them.

"Come and have a cuppa," said Alf. "Dorothy's sure to have the kettle on."

He was right.

"What's all this about a robbery at the Hall?" said Alf.

Pat had to tell the whole story again, from the beginning. He was getting a bit tired of it.

"Oh," said Pat, "I nearly forgot, with all this talk about the robbery. Peter Fogg's stuck with his motorbike broken down, about two miles back down the road. Do you think you could give him a hand, Ted?"

"No trouble," said Ted. "I'll pick him up when we've got this wood loaded."

"Thanks for the tea," said Pat. "Goodbye!"

Pat was on his way.

The next stop was Intake Farm.

"I hope I don't have to tell the story of the robbery all over again," said Pat.

But he didn't, because P.C. Selby was already there.

"Any news about the robbery?" said Pat.

"Good news and bad news," said P.C. Selby. "They've caught the robbers, on the road to Pencaster. But there's no sign of the collection of toy soldiers. Keep your eyes open for anything suspicious, won't you?"

"I certainly will," said Pat. "Cheerio!"

There were some letters and a magazine for George.

"Here's your *Poultry News*," said Pat.

"Now just look at that hen," said George, showing Pat a picture in his magazine. "It reminds me of an awful dream I had last night."

George told Pat how he had dreamed he was being chased by a giant hen! It had thought he was a chicken. And then he *was* a chicken. And he spread his wings and flew away . . .

"It's time I was flying away," said Pat. "I'm supposed to be collecting young Julian from school."

But Pat couldn't find Jess.

"Where has that cat got to?" said Pat.

"He might be after rabbits down the field," said George. "He likes my rabbits, does your Jess."

They went to look, and found Jess with his rear end sticking out of a rabbit-hole.

"Now then, Jess," said Pat, "what are you after?"

"I think he's got himself stuck," said George.

Pat took hold of Jess, and gently pulled. Jess went *pop* like a cork coming out of a bottle. A spray of sand and twigs came with him, and something small and heavy rolled into the grass. George picked it up, and looked at it.

"What's Jess found?" said Pat.

"Looks like one of these old tin soldiers," said George. "I used to have a box-full when I was a lad. It'll come up nice if I give it a polish."

"Did you say a *tin soldier*," said Pat.

"Yes. Why . . ."

"The robbery – you must have heard . . . hang on . . ."

Pat thrust his arm down the rabbit-hole as far as it would go, and brought out a plastic shopping bag tied up with string. He soon had the string off, and there were hundreds of toy soldiers.

"Jess has found the loot," said Pat. "The robbers must have hidden it on their way to Pencaster. They must have passed your gate."

"Clever cat," said George. "Even better than my hens. Mind you, they would have found them if Jess hadn't got there first."

"I must get these back to the Major," said Pat. "He will be pleased."

27

Pat put the bag of soldiers on the seat next to Jess.

"Keep an eye on these, Jess," he said. "Don't let them run away again."

But Jess would rather have found a rabbit or a mouse.

"Never mind, Jess. The Major will be so pleased to have his soldiers back, I'm sure he'll give you something nice."

Pat was on his way once more, back to Garner Hall.

He remembered to pick Julian up from school. On the way, he told him all about the robbery, and how Jess had found the soldiers down a rabbit-hole. They reached Garner Hall at last. Ted and the Major were still busy with that roof.

"What's the fellow doing with that scruffy plastic-bag?" said the Major, when he saw Pat. "Bless my eyes! It's my soldiers. My precious soldiers!"

And Pat told the whole story yet again!

"But it was Jess that found them," said Julian, "wasn't it?"

"It's a good place to hide something," said Ted, "down a rabbit-hole. Now who'd think of looking there?"

"We'd better be off home," said Pat. "Sara will think we've got lost."

"Take this with you," said Ted, giving Pat his copy of the *Pencaster Gazette*, "and make sure you look at page two."

"Thanks, Ted."

"I don't know why Ted wants me to read the paper," said Pat to Jess, as they drove along.

Julian couldn't wait to see what it was.

"It's about a reward," said Julian, "for anyone who finds the Major's soldiers. £500!"

"Well, I never," said Pat. "That'll buy a lot of fish for Jess. It's time we were on our way home, to tell Sara all our news."

"Let me tell her first," said Julian.